AWESOME SH*T
MY DRILL
SERGEANT SAID

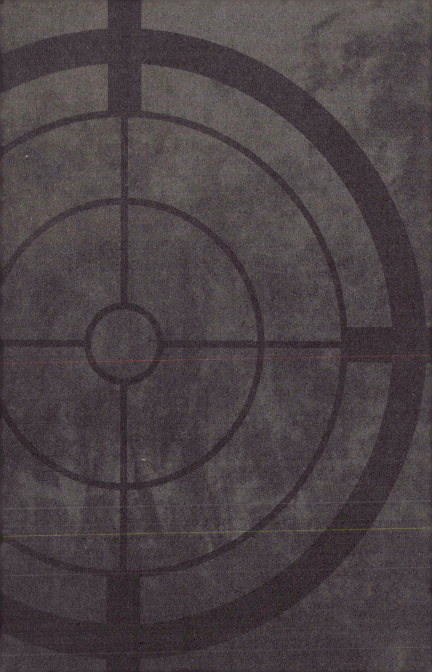

AWESOME SH*T MY DRILL SERGEANT SAID

Wit and Wisdom from America's Finest

DAN CADDY

DEY ST.
AN IMPRINT OF WILLIAM MORROW PUBLISHERS

DEY ST.

HarperCollins books may be purchased for educational, business,
or sales promotional use. For information please e-mail the Special
Markets Department at SPsales@harpercollins.com.

FIRST EDITION

Designed by Lorie Pagnozzi and Shannon Plunkett

Library of Congress Cataloging-in-Publication Data has been applied
for.

ISBN 978-0-06-235196-8

20 GV 19

THIS BOOK IS DEDICATED FIRST AND FOREMOST
TO ALL CURRENT AND FORMER DRILL SERGEANTS:
YOU HAVE SHAPED THE GENERATIONS OF
SOLDIERS WHO HAVE SERVED WITH DISTINCTION
IN BOTH PEACE AND WAR.

TO MY WIFE, LINDSEY, WHOSE SUPPORT AND
UNDERSTANDING DURING THE CRAZY TIMES
IS THE ONLY REASON ASMDSS IS STILL GOING
AND THIS BOOK EXISTS.

LAST BUT NOT LEAST, TO THE ADMINS AND STAFF
WHOSE ASSISTANCE, INSPIRATION, FRIENDSHIP,
AND CAMARADERIE MADE THIS BOOK POSSIBLE
FROM THE BEGINNING.

CONTENTS

AWESOME SH*T
MY DRILL
SERGEANT SAID

INTRODUCTION

Meet your drill sergeant, Private.

Even someone with zero knowledge of the military will see the fatigues and the "round brown" campaign hat and instantly know who they are looking at—a sight usually followed by a stab of uneasiness. Brought into the cultural mainstream by R. Lee Ermey in his masterful portrayal of a Marine Corps drill instructor in the film *Full Metal Jacket,* the drill sergeant is an immediately recognizable and iconic figure. Everyone has an idea in their head of what a drill sergeant is . . . and does. Often that image is focused on fear, aggression, pain, and discipline. And while it's true that a drill sergeant's larger-than-life persona and "motivational style" may incorporate some, or all, of those panic-inducing, gut-checking, strength-building forces, you might not know one other important thing . . . drill sergeants are some of the FUNNIEST people on the planet!

Those of you who have served in the military will have your own vivid memories of your drill sergeants (and know exactly what I'm talking about). And if you're anything like me, and the thousands of veterans I've talked with over the years, you can probably also speak to the impact that a drill sergeant has on your life after Basic Training has ended. This book, and the *Awesome Sh*t My Drill Sergeant Said* Facebook page that spawned it, collect the very best quotes, stories, lists, words of wisdom—and maybe a few insults—from America's finest drill sergeants. While they may not be there to uplift your spirits or compliment your wardrobe, drill sergeants have honed their ability to transform young men and women into professional disciplined warriors—and maybe have a good laugh (at you) while they do it.

THE CREEDS

THE DRILL SERGEANT CREED

I am a drill sergeant

I will assist each individual in their efforts to become a highly motivated, well disciplined, physically and mentally fit soldier, capable of defeating any enemy on today's modern battlefield.

I will instill pride in all I train. Pride in self, in the Army, and in country.

I will insist that each soldier meets and maintains the Army standards of military bearing and courtesy, consistent with the highest traditions of the U.S. Army.

I will lead by example, never requiring a soldier to attempt any task I would not do myself.

But first, last, and always, I am an American soldier. Sworn to defend the Constitution of the United States against all enemies, both foreign and domestic.

I am a drill sergeant.

THE SOLDIER'S CREED

I am an American soldier.

I am a warrior and a member of a team.

I serve the people of the United States, and live the Army values.

I will always place the mission first.

I will never accept defeat.

I will never quit.

I will never leave a fallen comrade.

I am disciplined, physically and mentally tough, trained and proficient in my warrior tasks and drills.

I always maintain my arms, my equipment, and myself.

I am an expert and I am a professional.

I stand ready to deploy, engage, and destroy the enemies of the United States of America in close combat.

I am a guardian of freedom and the American way of life.

I am an American soldier.

THE PRIVATE'S CREED

I am a private!

I am weak and have no heart.

I can never do the right thing or ever accept responsibility.

I will always place my feelings first!

I will never admit fault!

I will always quit!

I will always take the easy way out!

I am obnoxious, physically and mentally weak, immature, and potentially retarded.

I always maintain my profile, my sick call slips, and lack of motivation.

I wear my grenade bar.

I stand ready to fall out of, skip out on, or otherwise fail at PT.

I suck at life and will never try to better myself.

I am a private!

NOW YOU SEE WHY WE ARE ALWAYS PISSED OFF . . .

PART ONE
SHARK ATTACK

Welcome to Basic Training. Go ahead and thank your recruiter, your uncle, your own inner voice telling you to sign up—whoever it was—for paving the road to Basic. There is no turning back once you hit Reception. As a private, you arrive at the Reception Battalion, where you are processed in, get your immunizations, and are then issued your uniforms and equipment. And then, before you can call home to say you've changed your mind . . . Basic begins for real—with the Shark Attack.

In Basic Training parlance, a Shark Attack is just what you would probably imagine it to be—a veritable verbal feeding frenzy where drill sergeants are the sharks swarming around and unfortunate privates are their prey. The most unfortunate guppies in the group are the privates who have drawn attention to themselves for one or more transgressions. A true Shark Attack isn't complete yelling and screaming. It's a drill sergeant's job to bombard unlucky privates with as many stimuli as possible. The drill sergeants want to get an idea of who remains collected under pressure and who is easily flustered. Most important of all, a Shark Attack turns the world upside down for those privates, gives them their first real look at what is to come, and shows them just who will control every aspect of their lives for the next few months.

The most memorable of all Shark Attacks is Day Zero, which occurs when you leave Reception and you load up on transport, put your face in your duffel bag, and start counting the days until you're done with Basic. As you are dropped off at your Basic Training Company Area, your drill sergeants are there to greet you (nice, right?), lining the path from the bus to the Company Training Area. It is at that moment, as you pile out of the bus clutching your bags, that you most likely think, *What have I gotten myself into?*

ON DAY ZERO YOU LEARN NOT TO STARE AT YOUR DRILL SERGEANT . . .

"LOOK AT ME AGAIN AND I'LL SET YOU ON FIRE AND PUT YOU OUT WITH A FORK."

DRILL SERGEANTS DON'T SAY "DROP AND GIMME FIFTY" ANYMORE. THEY SAY . . .

"SHUT THE FUCK UP AND EAT SOME CONCRETE."

YOUR DRILL SERGEANT UNDERSTANDS YOU THINK
BASIC TRAINING IS HARD . . .

"YEAH, I BET THIS IS
A LOT HARDER THAN
SITTING IN YOUR
MOM'S BASEMENT,
SUCKING ON HER
TIT WHILE PLAYING
WORLD OF WARCRAFT,
YOU GOLEM-LOOKING
MOTHERFUCKER!"

"I AM THE FUCKING ALPHA AND FUCKING OMEGA OF YOUR FUCKING LIFE FOR THE NEXT TEN FUCKING WEEKS AND ONE FUCKING DAY, PRIVATE!"

DRILL SERGEANTS LOVE DIFFICULT CHALLENGES . . .

"HOW AM I SUPPOSED TO UNFUCK EIGHTEEN YEARS IN THREE MONTHS?"

DRILL SERGEANTS WANT TO TEACH YOU ABOUT TIME MANAGEMENT . . .

"WE'RE GONNA BE HERE EVERY HOUR, ON THE HOUR, FOR AN HOUR."

THEY ARE IDIOTS WHEN THEY ARRIVE . . .

I am a Reception Battalion drill sergeant. During the Reception process, the soldiers are taken to the PX (Post Exchange) to purchase their required items in preparation for Basic Combat Training. One of these items is a wristwatch. A soldier approached me, sounding serious:

SOLDIER: DRILL SERGEANT, WHICH WATCH DO WE BUY?

DS: SOLDIER, CHOOSE ONE OF THE AUTHORIZED WATCHES AND MOVE OUT.

SOLDIER: BUT, DRILL SERGEANT, WHICH ONE? THEY ALL HAVE DIFFERENT TIMES. WHICH WATCH IS SET TO THE CORRECT TIME?

DS: SOLDIER, IS THIS SUPPOSED TO BE FUNNY?

SOLDIER: NO, DRILL SERGEANT, I'M AFRAID IF I BUY THE WRONG WATCH I'LL BE LATE.

DS: THANK YOU, SOLDIER, I NEEDED THAT.

This is what we have to work with when the recruits arrive for Basic Training.

"PRIVATES, YOU'LL REALIZE THAT THERE ARE TWO WOMEN I WILL NEVER COMMENT ON. THOSE ARE YOUR MOMS AND YOUR WIVES. I DID FUCK ALL YOUR GIRLFRIENDS, THOUGH."

"IF YOU'RE HAVING
TROUBLE SLEEPING
TONIGHT, PRIVATES,
WHATEVER YOU DO, DON'T
THINK ABOUT THE FACT
THAT YOUR PARENTS ARE
PROBABLY HAVING SEX
IN YOUR OLD BEDROOM
BECAUSE YOUR
WATER-HEADED ASS IS
FINALLY GONE."

YOUR DRILL SERGEANT WANTS YOU
TO EAT, NOT TALK . . .

"IF I HEAR ONE MORE WORD OUT OF YOUR MOUTH, PRIVATES, I WILL PETER PAN ACROSS THE DFAC [DINING FACILITY] AND PUNCH A HOLE IN YOUR SOUL"

"PRIVATE, IF YOU EVER POINT YOUR FINGERS AGAIN, I WILL BITE THEM OFF LIKE BABY CARROTS."

DRILL SERGEANTS HATE BEING MISTAKEN FOR OFFICERS . . .

"DON'T CALL ME SIR, I WORK FOR A LIVING! AND MY PARENTS WERE NOT RELATED!"

DRILL SERGEANTS ARE THERE TO TEACH AND SUPPORT YOU . . .

"PRIVATE, DON'T EVER SALUTE ME AGAIN! I WILL SHOVE THAT HAND UP YOUR ASS SO FAR THAT YOU'LL NEVER NEED A PROSTATE EXAM!"

EVERYONE KNEW HIS NAME . . .

We arrived at Reception with nothing but the hopes and dreams promised by our recruiters, and the already in-stilled fear of the drill sergeants. There were plenty of people from all over the country. We had recruits from California, Mississippi, Connecticut, Louisiana, Virginia, Vermont, even Hawaii. This particular private was named Takeu***chit, a good kid from Hawaii of Hawaiian Japa-nese descent.

One day during Reception we were served some pret-ty rough food at the chow hall. Once we were finished with everything for the day, we were released back to the barracks. For some strange reason the food did not sit so well with everybody in the platoon, so every single pri-vate and their mom was taking a dump in the latrine. Ev-ery single stall was being utilized with somebody cutting some major weight. Private Takeu***chit was the only one left latrine-less. Out of sheer desperation he decided to take a shit on the emergency stairwell in the barracks and to hide it behind a trash can.

Later that evening we were back in the barracks and somebody started smelling a foul odor in the air. "Some-thing smells like SHIT," yelled one of the privates. "What the fuck is that smell?" yelled another.

The smell was so bad that people were seen leaving the barracks to go outside, just to give some relief to their burning nostrils. Enter a drill sergeant: "Why the fuck is nobody in their bunks! It is way past lights-out!"

One of the privates yelled, "Somebody took a shit in the barracks, DS!"

After the privates had spent hours doing push-ups, the culprit, Private Takeu***chit, was found and made to clean up the mess.

Fast-forward to the first day of Basic Training. We met our drill sergeants for the first time. Shark Attack Central! Knife hands flying, round browns swirling in a cyclone of noise, hate, and intimidation. One of the drill sergeants stopped suddenly and looked at Private Takeu***chit. He yelled out, *"Holy fuck, battle! It's him! It's him, it's him!"*

The cyclone of round browns stops and they all converged on the now extremely nervous Private Takeu***chit. The DS pulled out his phone and took a picture with him. "Oh, shit, battle, his name . . . it's Private Take-A-Shit!" The whole platoon erupted in laughter. Bad idea . . . the DS's immediately dropped us all and smoked the dog snot out of us for breaking discipline.

The goal of Basic Training is to go as long as possible before the drill sergeants know your name. Private Takeu***chit failed at that on DAY ONE. All throughout Basic Training, Private Takeu***chit from that point on was known as Private Take-A-Shit!

DRILL SERGEANTS WANT YOU TO UNDERSTAND
YOU'RE NOT A LITTLE BABY ANYMORE . . .

"YOUR MOTHER'S TIT ONLY STRETCHES SO FAR."

DRILL SERGEANTS WANT YOU TO EAT LIKE
A GROWN-UP . . .

"BRING THE BANANA TO YOUR FACE, PRIVATES, NOT YOUR FACE TO THE BANANA."

DRIVING LESSONS . . .

DRILL SERGEANT: WHO IN HERE CAN DRIVE A STICK?

PRIVATE: I CAN, DS!

DS: OUTSTANDING! (DS HANDS OVER A MOP.) DRIVE THIS AROUND THE DAMN FLOOR TILL YOU COULD FEED YOUR MAMA ON IT.

"I WANT THAT TOILET SEAT SO CLEAN I CAN MAKE A SANDWICH ON IT."

DRILL SERGEANTS HAVE A UNIQUE SENSE OF SMELL . . .

"Y'ALL NEED TO CLEAN THESE BARRACKS . . . MOTHERFUCKER SMELLS LIKE A GOAT IN AN OVERCOAT."

DRILL SERGEANTS WANT YOU TO SPEAK CLEARLY . . .

"IS THAT A 'YES, DRILL SERGEANT,' 'NO, DRILL SERGEANT,' OR A 'FUCK YOU, DRILL SERGEANT'?!"

DRILL SERGEANTS UNDERSTAND TIME CONSTRAINTS . . .

"I CAN SHOWER, FEED MYSELF, FEED A BABY, AND MAKE A BABY ALL IN UNDER TEN MINUTES. YOU KNUCKLEHEADS SURE AS SHIT CAN EAT A GODDAMN MEAL IN TEN MINUTES."

BUT DRILL SERGEANTS EXPECT YOU TO
DRESS YOURSELF . . .

"IT LOOKS LIKE A BIG CAN OF FUCK BLEW UP ALL OVER YOUR UNIFORM."

DRILL SERGEANTS WANT TO HELP YOU GET WHERE YOU NEED TO BE . . .

"I WILL PERSONALLY BUILD A STAIRCASE TO THROW YOU DOWN, PRIVATE!"

I DIDN'T WANT TO JOIN THE ARMY . . .

The first week of Basic the drill sergeant asked if we had any questions. We had one kid who raised his hand.

KID: WHAT IF YOU AREN'T SUPPOSED TO BE HERE?

DS: WHAT?

KID: I DIDN'T WANT TO JOIN THE ARMY, BUT MY DAD MADE ME.

Our DS pulled him out of the formation and had him stand in the rear. When we got back to the barracks, DS called him into the office. All was quiet for a minute, and then we all flinched as the DS dropped the bomb on this poor kid. He yelled and berated him for five minutes straight and didn't hold anything back.

About four weeks later, I pulled security with the kid while the rest of the platoon had rifle training. He had scored forty out of forty on BRM (Basic Rifle Marksmanship) and I got thirty-nine, so the two of us got guard duty. A DS drove out to bring us lunch and check on us.

He hopped out of the car and asked, "You guys been sleeping?"

US: NO, DRILL SERGEANT!

DS: WHY NOT? THERE ARE TWO OF YOU. TAKE TURNS.

Later that afternoon, I asked the guy about his chat with the DS that first week. I told him that I was impressed with his perfect score on the range and pointed out that he seemed to be doing okay even though he didn't want to be there.

He told me I couldn't tell anyone, but here is what the DS said to him:

[QUIETLY, WITH THE DOOR CLOSED.]

"SON, I KNOW THIS IS A BIT TOUGH ON YOU, BUT I THINK YOU HAVE WHAT IT TAKES. IF YOU START TO FEEL TOO OVERWHELMED, YOU COME AND SEE ME, QUIETLY, NOT IN FRONT OF EVERYONE ELSE, AND I'LL WORK WITH YOU. MEANWHILE, I HAVE THIRTY-FOUR OTHER MEN OUT THERE WHO NEED TO HEAR THIS, SO JUST SIT BACK AND RELAX AND IGNORE ME FOR A MINUTE . . ."

Then the tirade began.

Twenty-five years later I still remember that DS fondly. He got the best out of us, without being a jerk.

DRILL SERGEANTS MAKE THEIR OWN
AWESOME RULES . . .

"THEY SAY I CAN'T CURSE . . . FUCK THAT!"

DRILL SERGEANTS WANT TO SET YOU
UP FOR SUCCESS . . .

"I'M ABOUT TO
FUCK START YOUR
LIFE, PRIVATE."

DRILL SERGEANTS HAVE AN EXTENSIVE VOCABULARY . . .

"YOU LOOK LIKE A SPILLED BUCKET OF FUCK! I DON'T EVEN KNOW WHAT THAT MEANS, BUT IT'S THE ONLY THING I CAN THINK OF THAT ACCURATELY DESCRIBES WHAT GOES THROUGH MY MIND WHEN I SEE YOUR OXYGEN-THIEVING FACE!"

TOP 10 THINGS YOU ARE MORE FUCKED UP THAN

10. A screen door on a submarine.

9. An Amish electrician.

8. A pregnant trapeze artist.

7. A one-legged cat trying to bury shit on a frozen pond.

6. Polio.

5. Clown porn in church.

4. An albino trying to hitchhike in a snowstorm.

3. A nun doing power squats nude in a cucumber field.

2. Helen Keller using an iPod.

1. A football bat hitting a golf puck into a soccer basket wearing steel-toed flip-flops eating spaghetti with a carving knife.

DRILL SERGEANTS LOVE TO COMPLIMENT YOUR LOOKS . . .

"YOU LOOK LIKE YOUR MAMA FED YOU WITH A FUCKIN' SLINGSHOT, PRIVATE!"

AND YOUR PERSONAL HYGIENE . . .

"WHAT DID YOU SHAVE WITH, PRIVATE? A BOWL OF MILK AND AN ANGRY CAT?"

DRILL SERGEANTS WANT YOU TO THANK THE RIGHT PERSON FOR GETTING YOU TO BASIC TRAINING . . .

"DON'T THANK ME, THANK YOUR MOTHER FOR NOT SWALLOWING."

"DON'T THANK ME, THANK YOUR RECRUITER."

"DON'T THANK ME, THANK YOUR DAD FOR NOT FIRING YOU INTO A NAPKIN."

HE FOLLOWED ORDERS . . .

We had all just completed the three-minute phone call home we were given when we first got to Basic to let our families know we were safe. A few minutes after we all returned to our bay, a drill sergeant came barging in yelling "FUCK" left and right and having us all toe the line. His veins were bulging out of his neck and forehead.

DS: WHICH ONE OF YOU FUCKING IDIOTS TOLD YOUR MOM WHAT I'VE BEEN SAYING?

    [THE PRIVATES GIVE BACK BLANK STARES.]

DS: WHICH DUMB FUCK ACTUALLY THANKED HIS MOM FOR NOT SWALLOWING HIM?!

    [ONE PRIVATE SLOWLY RAISES HIS HAND.]

DS: WHAT THE FUCK DID YOU DO THAT FOR?

PRIVATE: BECAUSE YOU TOLD ME TO, DRILL SERGEANT?

    [DS FACE-PALMS.]

DS: DO PUSH-UPS, PRIVATE. JUST . . . PUSH.

"YOU PRIVATES ARE SOFTER THAN A SNEAKERFUL OF PUPPY SHIT!"

DRILL SERGEANTS HAVE AWESOME
SPECIAL POWERS . . .

"I CAN HEAR A RAT PISS ON COTTON FROM A MILE AWAY."

DRILL SERGEANTS ARE DEFINITELY
STRONGER THAN YOU . . .

"PRIVATES, IF YOU EVER SEE ME WRESTLING A BEAR IN THE WOODS . . . YOU BETTER COME RUNNING, BECAUSE THE BEAR . . . IT'S IN TROUBLE."

YOUR WORST NIGHTMARE . . .

It was our first day in Basic, and we had just arrived, and after the initial Shark Attack we were told to grab our bags and move out to our bay and put our things on our bunks and stand toe-to-line. As we were standing there, Drill Sergeant J proceeded to introduce himself as the baddest mo-fo in the land. While our attention was focused on him, Drill Sergeant H snuck in the back door and went into the latrine. He tossed a Snickers bar into the toilet and poured a little of his "mountain dew" over it. Immediately he came running out of the latrine yelling, "Which one of you mother#$*#@ took a shit in my latrine and didn't flush it? No one? I guess God Himself came down from heaven and chose my latrine to do His business. EVERY ONE OF YOU, LATRINE, NOW!"

All sixty-four of us quickly piled into that little latrine, looking around, trying to determine who was the culprit. Now DS H was standing in the stall screaming at us, and all of us were silent and glancing around nervously. Without hesitation, he reached his hand into the toilet, picked up the "turd" and took a bite of it, then spit it in one unlucky private's face. All of us were mortified and speechless. He said, "I don't know what you pussies think you got yourself into, but I'm going to become your worst nightmare."

"I'D RATHER BE ON HAND-JOB DUTY AT THE PENTAGON THAN BE HERE LOOKING AT YOU STUPID, PATHETIC, MOTHERLESS FUCKS."

DRILL SERGEANTS THINK YOU HAVE POTENTIAL . . .

"JESUS CHRIST, PRIVATE! YOU LOOK LIKE THE AFTERBIRTH OF A CLUSTER FUCK!"

SERGEANTS DON'T WANT YOU TO MOVE AT THE
POSITION OF ATTENTION . . .

"I DON'T CARE IF A
SNAKE IS BITING YOUR
TESTICLES, YOU DO NOT
MOVE AT THE POSITION
OF ATTENTION!"

"I DON'T CARE IF A
PTERODACTYL STARTS
FUCKING YOUR FACE,
YOU DON'T MOVE AT
THE POSITION OF
ATTENTION. YOU LET
HIM FINISH."

"STAND THE FUCK STILL, YOU TWITCHY SHIT KNUCKLE!"

I HAD NO IDEA WHAT TO EXPECT . . .

I didn't know the first thing about the Army when I joined. I was a pudgy, five-foot-plus-your-dick-in-inches E-nothing—basically an enlisted member of the military with no authority over anything or anybody. I didn't play Call of Duty and I wasn't a big fan of war movies, so I had no idea what to expect going into Basic Combat Training (BCT). Honestly, I thought it would be camping, classes, and some exercising.

I had never been so wrong.

Drill Sergeant K was a six-foot-three-inch infantry-man, a staff sergeant (SSG), and an all-around American badass. My first time meeting him was during the brutal introduction to Basic Training known as Shark Attack on Day Zero. I remember having my name called out as a signal to join the rest of my platoon, and I had to run past him in a narrow passageway. His first words to me were "DON'T YOU FUCKIN' TEST ME!" The explosive nature of the words and the volume in which they were yelled literally knocked me to the ground. Of course I ended up in his platoon.

Let me be clear: you DID NOT FUCK with DS K. I learned this the hard way in week six. We were all up bright and early, marching to take the second Army Phys-ical Fitness Test (APFT) of the cycle. It was absolutely

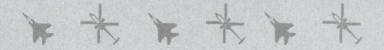

freezing and a dense fog combined with the complete blackness of the night. Only our reflective belts distinguished us from utter darkness as we marched toward our PT field.

Now, in no way was I a PT stud. My goal was simply to pass the APFT by the end of the cycle, not max out. On this specific test I was able to get through the push-ups and sit-ups just fine, but then the two-mile-run event arrived and I was shaking in my size-nine sneakers. I'd never done well in the two-mile, even though I ran hard out every morning in Assigned Group Runs.

Anyway, before I knew it, the event had started and I paced myself through the first couple of laps (eight laps = two miles). Around lap three, I tried to pump myself up, saying "C'mon, halfway there, you can do it," that kind of shit. But before long I was sweating, shaking my head, and muttering to myself like a priest getting a lap dance.

By lap five I was suffering BAD, almost all words of encouragement were lost to me, and I could tell my body was starting to shut down. But then, for whatever reason (it escapes me to this day), I began to vocalize two simple words, repeating them again and again to myself: "Oh yeah."

Not even NBC's best writers could come up with the shit that came next.

As I muttered "Oh yeah" over and over again to myself, I failed to realize two things: (1) I was beginning to say it louder and louder; and (2) I was running side by side with DS K, who was pacing for slower privates like me. Then, without realizing what I was doing, I bellowed out, louder than ever, "OH YEAH!"

From behind I hear DS K shout, "WHAT ARE YOU? THE FUCKING KOOL-AID GUY?!"

Now, at that point, most privates would respond "DS, no, DS" and keep running. Or at the very least, all non-mouth-breathing privates with at least half of a brain would just shut the hell up and refrain from saying what I was about to say.

Instead of changing course, I amped up. I raised my head and bellowed with all my might, from the abyss of my lungs, "OHHHH YYEAAHHHHHH," and kicked my ass into maximum overdrive.

This is where it gets hazy. Now I sure as hell didn't purposefully disrespect a DS who I looked up to and still do to this day . . . so why did I say it? I know it wasn't because I mistook him for a private, because he had a voice that sounded like hatred and sharp weapons (mostly hatred).

For the remainder of the run I sprinted, not daring to turn and look behind me. With every step, I had the im-

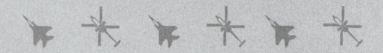

age of DS K closing in on me like a lion on a baby gazelle, ready to grind my face into the asphalt and leave a bloody skid mark as a warning to all privates everywhere.

Luckily, that didn't happen, and I finished at 13:56, two and a half minutes faster than I had ever run it before. And then, of course, I puked at the finish line more than Tara Reid did on her twenty-first birthday.

"I KNOW A LOT OF YOU COME FROM A LONG LINE OF WINDOW LICKERS. BUT TODAY I NEED YOU TO PUT YOUR CRAYONS BACK IN YOUR BOX AND PUT AWAY YOUR HELMETS AND STOP CHEWING ON YOUR FOOTLOCKERS."

"I DO NOT DISCRIMINATE. IF MY OWN MOTHER WAS IN BASIC TRAINING, I WOULD SMOKE HER ASS TOO!"

BUT YOUR DRILL SERGEANT WANTS YOU TO KNOW
YOU DO NOT IMPRESS HIM . . .

"PRIVATE,
EVERY ONCE IN
A WHILE A SOLDIER
COMES THROUGH
HERE THAT GIVES ME
A GLIMMER OF
HOPE FOR THE FUTURE
OF OUR ARMY.
YOU'RE NOT THAT PRIVATE.
AS A MATTER OF FACT,
I DIE A LITTLE
INSIDE EACH TIME YOU
ATTEMPT A TASK."

PART TWO
SINK OR SWIM

When you arrive at Basic Training you are a civilian, but more importantly you are an individual. In civilian life it's normal to think about yourself and focus just on what you need, but this is not how things are done in the Army. The smallest military unit is a two-person, "Battle Buddy" team. The saying is "two is one, and one is none." That's a major adjustment for most privates.

For an entering private, the focus in "Red Phase" is to shock you, shake you up, and break you down to your base level—all the while training you in the basics of individual soldier skills. Think of it as if the drill sergeant is a painter. When privates arrive, they are a canvas, only one that is messy, unorganized, and covered in the random junk they've picked up over a lifetime of doing things the civilian way as opposed to the Army way. Not the type of art anyone's hanging in their home! Before your drill sergeant can begin to paint you as a professional soldier he needs to wipe that canvas clean. Reception, Shark Attack, Red Phase . . . all are means to getting a clean canvas to work with.

As privates move into the White and Blue Phases of Basic Training, the painting begins in earnest. Among the most important goals is to get you thinking not of yourself, but of your fellow soldier, your squad, your platoon, and how your actions affect them and the overall success of whatever task is at hand. Teamwork is the key. You are now learning the major aspects of soldiering, namely shooting, moving, and communicating . . . all done under the watchful eye of drill sergeants.

In order to complete one phase and move on to the next, all soldiers must be tested and show that they are able to carry out the required tasks in that phase, as well as be free of disciplinary and performance problems.

At this point in the training, privates are starting to get used to the routine and the differences between civilian life and Army life. Take standing in line, for example. As a civilian, you would most likely be moving, talking, playing with your doggone smartphone, or some other undisciplined crap. As a private, you stand in line at the position of parade rest with your eyes forward. No moving, no talking. When it is time to move forward in the line, you come to the position of attention, move forward, and then snap smartly back to parade rest.

For civilians, a meal is usually a calm, leisurely affair

where you have all the time you want to eat. As a private, YOU HAVE SEVEN MINUTES TO SHOVEL THOSE GROCERIES DOWN YOUR THROAT AND GET THE HELL OUT OF MY DINING FACILITY!

As a civilian, when you fuck up . . . you might be punished. As a recruit, when you fuck up . . . your entire platoon has the dog shit smoked out of them while you stand there at the position of attention and watch.

These are just a few examples of the culture shock that is taking place. At this point drill sergeants have an idea of who is who—who the natural leaders are, who the slackers are, who the smartasses are, and most importantly . . . who the guys trying to stay under the radar and skate through are. Rest assured, they have a plan for all of the characters listed above, as you will see in this chapter.

SINKING IS NOT AN OPTION . . .

PRIVATE: WHAT HAPPENS IF WE DON'T KNOW HOW TO SWIM, DRILL SERGEANT?

DRILL SERGEANT: I SUGGEST YOU HOLD YOUR BREATH AND RUN LIKE HELL WHEN YOU GET TO THE BOTTOM. ANY OTHER QUESTIONS?

YOUR DRILL SERGEANT THINKS YOU'RE MAKING
PROGRESS AT BASIC . . .

"WELL, FUCKIN' CONGRATULATIONS, YOU ARE NO LONGER A SOUP SANDWICH. YOU, PRIVATE, HAVE BEEN PROMOTED TO A CHICKEN NOODLE HOAGIE!"

BUT YOUR DRILL SERGEANT WANTS YOU TO KNOW
WHAT HAPPENS TO HIM WHEN YOU FUCK UP . . .

"TOE THE LINE,
ASSHOLES! GODDAMMIT,
SECOND PLATOON!
YOU MAKE ME SICK!
YOU KEEP FAILING ME!
YOU KEEP FAILING
YOURSELVES!
YOU CAN'T SHOOT SHIT!
YOU CAN'T GET
READY ON TIME!
YOU GET ME SO PISSED
OFF THAT LAST NIGHT
I WENT HOME AND KICKED
MY WIFE'S DOG.
HAD TO SLEEP ON THE
FUCKING COUCH!

I CAN'T DO THAT SHIT
BECAUSE SHE GETS
PISSED AT ME.
WHEN SHE GETS PISSED
AT ME, I TAKE IT
OUT ON PRIVATES.
WHEN I TAKE IT
OUT ON PRIVATES,
I GET DEMOTED.
WHEN I GET DEMOTED,
MY WIFE DIVORCES
ME BECAUSE I CAN'T
PAY FOR SHIT!
STRAIGHTEN OUT YOUR ACT,
SECOND PLATOON!"

**DRILL SERGEANTS KNOW HOW TO LET YOU KNOW
WHEN YOU ARE WRONG . . .**

"PRIVATE, YOU'RE LIKE BANGING A FAT CHICK IN AN ELEVATOR. WRONG ON SO MANY LEVELS!"

DRILL SERGEANTS JUST WANT TO ENCOURAGE
SELF-IMPROVEMENT . . .

"YOU SERIOUSLY CAN'T DO ONE PULL-UP, FATTY? I BET YOU JACK OFF TO COOKBOOKS!"

DRILL SERGEANTS ARE THE ULTIMATE
PROBLEM SOLVERS...

"I AM GOING TO INSTALL A WINDOW IN YOUR STOMACH SO YOU CAN SEE WHERE YOU'RE GOING WITH YOUR HEAD UP YOUR ASS!"

WE PULLED OUR HEADS OUT . . .

Upon finally arriving at our Basic Training Company, and following the initial Shark Attack, we found ourselves standing in formation in front of the senior drill sergeant. He wanted to set the proper tone from the beginning. Facing the formation, he gave some odd commands.

DS: PLATOON, ATTENTION!

(PLATOON STANDS AT ATTENTION.)

DS: NOW BEND OVER LIKE YOU'RE GOING TO BITE YOUR FUCKING CROTCH!

(EVERYONE IS BENT OVER.)

DS: NOW, ON THREE, STAND UP AS FAST AS YOU CAN AND YELL "POP!"

PLATOON: ONE! . . . TWO! . . . THREE! POP!

DS: PRIVATES, DO YOU KNOW WHAT THAT WAS THE SOUND OF?

PLATOON: NO, DS! WHAT?

DS: THE SOUND OF YOU PULLING YOUR HEAD OUT OF YOUR ASS!

**DRILL SERGEANTS LOVE PAYING YOU
COMPLIMENTS ON YOUR PHYSIQUE . . .**

"PRIVATE, YOU LOOK LIKE A CAN OF BISCUITS THAT'S JUST BEEN POPPED OPEN."

DRILL SERGEANTS ARE EXPERTS AT
JUDGING BODY MASS . . .

"YOU'RE NOT OVERWEIGHT. YOU'RE OVERFAT!"

DRILL SERGEANTS CARE ABOUT YOUR LONG-TERM HEALTH . . .

"SOLDIER, IF I CHECKED YOUR DOG TAGS RIGHT NOW, I'M GUESSING YOUR BLOOD TYPE WOULD BE DIABETES! GET A SALAD!"

"YOU'RE GONNA BE SO RIPPED BY THE TIME I'M DONE WITH YOU, YOUR NIPPLES ARE GONNA HAVE SIX-PACKS!"

DRILL SERGEANTS JUST WANT YOU TO
MAKE GOOD CHOICES . . .

"PRIVATE, LIFE IS LIKE A BOX OF CHOCOLATES. IT LASTS LONGER IF YOU'RE NOT FAT."

TOP TEN THINGS YOU ARE SLOWER THAN

10. Turtle shit going uphill sideways.

9. The VA.

8. Snail snot in peanut butter.

7. Stephen Hawking with a dead battery.

6. A one-fingered whore at a circle jerk.

5. A West Virginia prom date.

4. A monkey trying to fuck its way to the center of a coconut.

3. Helen Keller in a spelling bee.

2. A midget climbing a beanstalk.

1. A snail riding a sloth swimming uphill through molasses in January.

DRILL SERGEANTS CAN DESCRIBE YOU IN WAYS
YOU NEVER THOUGHT POSSIBLE . . .

"YOU ARE THAT
KIND OF GUY WHO
WIPES HIS ASS FROM
BACK TO FRONT,
GETS SHIT ON HIS
BALLS, AND WONDERS
WHY NO ONE WILL
BLOW HIM. WE ARE
GOING TO FIX YOU,
PRIVATE!"

YOUR DRILL SERGEANTS WANT YOU TO FEEL PRETTY . . .

"YOU LOOK LIKE SOMEONE FUCKING SET YOU ON FIRE AND THEN DECIDED TO PUT YOU OUT WITH A GODDAMN WET CHAIN."

CREATIVE TEACHING METHODS . . .

Drill Sergeant C was the most creative DS in the company. It also happened that he was the one most easily pissed off, which allowed him more chances at being creative. But what he hated most was privates falling asleep when he was talking. We were in the war room receiving some sort of instruction from DS C when Pvt. Fuckup starts to nod off. DS C saw this and silently walked over to the unsuspecting Pvt. and screamed.

"DOES IT SOUND LIKE I'M SINGING YOU A FUCK-ING LULLABY, PRIVATE? IS MY VOICE SOOTHING?"

Pvt. Fuckup stands to parade rest faster than he can open his eyes. "NO, DS!"

"THEN WHY THE FUCK ARE YOU SLEEPING DURING MY INSTRUCTION?"

"I . . . I dunno, DS!"

"BULLSHIT. YOU FELL ASLEEP BECAUSE YOU MUST BE TIRED. LET'S FIX THAT."

At this point DS C instructed Pvt. Fuckup to go to his room, dress in his PTs, and bring his bunk into the war room. DS C continued his instructions until Pvt. Fuckup finished bringing the bunk into the war room.

"Now lay the fuck down in your bunk and shut your fucking eyes."

DS C began to sing a lullaby in his ears.

"Rockaby, Private, in the war room, falling asleep, FRONT LEANING REST POSITION MOVE," and then he had him in his bunk, in the leaning rest, fake-snoring with his eyes closed for the duration of our time in the war room.

DRILL SERGEANTS REALLY WANT TO BE FRIENDS WITH YOU. . .

"I'M GONNA CALL YOU BASKIN, PRIVATE, 'CAUSE YOU'RE ALL THIRTY-ONE FLAVORS OF FUCKED UP."

"YOU'RE ABOUT AS SHARP AS THE LEADING EDGE ON A BOWLING BALL."

REMEMBER, YOUR DRILL SERGEANT KNOWS THE MEANING OF LIFE . . .

"LIFE SUCKS; GET A HELMET!"

HE JUST AIN'T RIGHT . . .

I had a private one cycle that I will never forget. We drill sergeants joke around about privates being stupid and call them slow and dumb, etc., but I'm pretty well convinced that this kid actually had something seriously wrong with him. We had one incredibly frustrating day of Basic Rifle Marksmanship (BRM) where I had to give this kid one-on-one special time on the Weaponeer, and I shit you not, it was like he broke down each of the fundamentals of marksmanship and did exactly the opposite, on purpose. I walked up behind him and stared at the back of his head, seriously contemplating where I would hide his body that evening after I killed him, and I noticed that he had two horizontal scars on the back of his head— side by side like two big dashes.

ME: PRIVATE, WHAT THE FUCK HAPPENED TO THE BACK OF YOUR HEAD?

PRIVATE (IN A SOUTHERN DRAWL): DRILL SERGEANT, MY MAMA HIT ME IN THE BACK OF THE HEAD WITH A CLAW HAMMER WHEN I WAS A KID.

ME: HOLY SHIT, PRIVATE! I GUESS YOU CAME BY IT HONESTLY: EVEN YOUR MOM CAN'T COMPLETE A SIMPLE TASK TO STANDARD . . .

"PRIVATES, Y'ALL HAVE BEEN EYE-FUCKING ME SO MUCH LATELY I THINK THERE IS A POSSIBILITY I MAY BE FUCKING PREGNANT."

"QUIT EYE-FUCKING ME, PRIVATE! DO YOU WANT TO HAVE EYE BABIES?"

"LOOK AT ME AGAIN, AND I WILL TEAR YOUR FACE OFF AND WEAR IT TO THE NEXT FORMATION!"

"IF ANOTHER ONE OF YOU FUCKFACES SPITS IN MY FORMATION, I'M GONNA MAKE YOU PICK IT UP AND PUT IT IN YOUR POCKET!"

**BUT DRILL SERGEANTS ARE OKAY
WITH SOME TEARS . . .**

"YOUR TEARS ARE
LIKE JET FUEL TO ME:
IF I COULD BOTTLE
THEM, I WOULD TAKE
THEM HOME."

"ARE YOU CRYING?
PLEASE KEEP CRYING—
I LIKE TO LICK THE
TEARS OFF OF
PRIVATES' FACES. IT
SUSTAINS ME."

THERE'S NO CRYING AT BASIC . . .

One night, about two weeks into the cycle, Drill Sergeant B, the meanest motherfucker I ever met, walked into our room and said, "Has the crying stopped at night yet, Privates?" To which all of us replied in frightened voices, "Yes, Drill Sergeant . . ." He quickly snapped back, "Good, Privates."

He turned to leave the room and then he did an about-face, came back in, and said, "Privates, I'm always watching you. When you go to sleep, I'm there in your nightmares. Even when you graduate and you join the big Army, I'll still be watching you, waiting for you to fuck up so I can smoke the shit out of you. In ten years, if you see me walking down the street, I will see you, see the look of fear in your eyes, and know you were one of my privates. So I suggest if you ever see me, you do an about-face and run as fast as you can. But it doesn't matter how far you run; I'll find you. I will find you and smoke the everloving shit out of you." He then headed toward the door and left us.

Right as the door was about to slam shut we heard him say, "Sweet dreams, Privates."

DRILL SERGEANTS KNOW HOW TO
DEAL WITH BULLIES . . .

"WANT TO STOP A BULLY? MAN THE FUCK UP AND PUNCH THAT MOTHERFUCKER IN THE THROAT! PROBLEM SOLVED."

SHOWERING IS NOT OPTIONAL . . .

My drill sergeant was doing a routine inspection when suddenly I hear:

"WHAT THE UNHOLY FUCK IS THAT SMELL, PRIVATES?! IT SMELLS LIKE Y'ALL DECIDED TO USE YOUR GODDAMNED WALL LOCKERS AS SHITTERS!"

He continues on, and not two seconds later I hear:

"ALL RIGHT, SERIOUSLY, PRIVATES, NO MORE BULLSHIT-TING, THE FUCK IS THAT SMELL?"

A PRIVATE SAYS, "DRILL SERGEANT, PRIVATE X DOESN'T PERFORM PERSONAL HYGIENE, DRILL SERGEANT!"

DS: THE FUCK DID YOU SAY?

So the drill sergeant walks up to the now freshly named Private Shower and says:

"YOU NASTY LITTLE FUCK! YOU SMELL WORSE THAN A THAI HOOKER ON TWO-FOR-ONE NIGHT! I MEAN, HOLY HELL, PRIVATE, I HAVE BEEN IN SHIT, AND I'D RATHER BE KNEE-DEEP IN IT THAN SMELL YOUR UNSANITARY, INHUMAN, UNWORTHY, REPULSIVE ASS! FROM NOW ON, PRIVATE, WE'RE GOING TO HAVE A SIGN-IN SHEET BY THE SHOWERS, AND YOU WILL HAVE TO SHOWER WITH EVERY OTHER PISS-FOR-BRAIN PRIVATE HERE. YOUR NAME WILL

BE FIRST EVERY FUCKING NIGHT FOR THE REST OF THE CYCLE OR I SWEAR TO WHATEVER GOD YOU BELIEVE IN I WILL HAVE YOU DOING LOW CRAWLS IN THE PIT UNTIL YOU SHIT MOTOR OIL!"

DRILL SERGEANTS KNOW HOW TO
GET YOUR ATTENTION . . .

"HEY! YOU WITH THE FACE!"

DRILL SERGEANTS WANT YOU TO HAVE SITUATIONAL AWARENESS . . .

"YOU PRIVATES ARE SO CLUELESS YOU WOULDN'T NOTICE A GIANT PURPLE DINOSAUR CLIMBING OUT OF MY ASS."

YOUR DRILL SERGEANT HAS PLENTY OF RULES TO LIVE BY . . .

"REMEMBER, PRIVATES, THAT THERE IS ONLY ONE RULE THAT YOU SHOULD FOLLOW NO MATTER THE SITUATION: IF IT DON'T SMELL RIGHT, DON'T EAT IT."

DRILL SERGEANTS CAN HELP YOU IMPROVE YOUR VOCABULARY . . .

"**IF YOU ARE LOOKING FOR SYMPATHY, YOU CAN FIND IT IN THE DICTIONARY BETWEEN 'SHIT' AND 'SYPHILIS,' WHERE IT BELONGS.**"

AND DRILL SERGEANTS KNOW
A LOT ABOUT MUSIC . . .

"YOU PRIVATES SOUND WORSE THAN AN OCTOPUS TRYING TO FUCK A SET OF BAGPIPES, SWEET BABY JESUS!"

"PRIVATE, I CAN EAT A BOWL OF ALPHABET SOUP AND SHIT OUT A BETTER QUESTION THAN THAT."

DRILL SERGEANTS CARE ABOUT THE FUNDAMENTALS OF MARKSMANSHIP . . .

"THAT TRIGGER IS NOT YOUR DICK. QUIT JERKIN' IT!"

A CURE FOR THE JITTERS . . .

There was a private who was always jittery and nervous. It was about the fifth week in, and this private was in formation. He had snakes showing (boot laces hanging out) and the drill sergeant walked right up to him.

DRILL SERGEANT: GODDAMMIT. EVERY TIME THERE IS SOMETHING WITH YOU.

The private just stood there and started to shiver a little.

DS: JESUS, ARE YOU FUCKING SHAKING ALREADY, PRIVATE? WHAT IS YOUR FUCKING ISSUE?

PVT.: I WILL FIX THE BOOT, DS!

DS: PRIVATE, WHEN WAS THE LAST TIME YOU JERKED OFF?

PVT.: UHHH, I HAVEN'T, DS.

DS: HOLY FUCKING SHIT, PRIVATE. THAT IS YOUR GODDAMN FUCKING ISSUE RIGHT THERE. YOU ARE ALL BUILT UP INSIDE AND YOU CAN'T FUCKING THINK STRAIGHT. YOU GOTTA GET THAT SHIT OUT OF YOU. TAKE YOUR ASS UPSTAIRS RIGHT NOW TO THE FUCKING LATRINE. START YANKING ONE OUT. YOU HAVE TEN MINUTES. GO!

The private just stood there. He had no idea what to do.

DS: GET THE FUCK UPSTAIRS RIGHT NOW TO THE LATRINE OR I WILL FUCKING KEEP YOU IN THE FRONT LEANING REST UNTIL HELL FUCKING FREEZES OVER!

The private took off running as fast as he could to the stairs. The DS had the biggest shit-eating grin on his face.

After a few minutes, the DS walked over to the main office and yelled in there: "Hey, battle! I just did a head count and we are missing a private. Can you go upstairs and check the latrines to see if someone is hiding?" We were doing everything within our power to keep from laughing as the other DS went up the stairs. Everyone knew what was going to happen.

The windows were open to vent out the bays and all of a sudden we heard: *"WHAT THE FUCK ARE YOU DOING, PRIVATE!? HOLY FUCKING SHIT! PUT YOUR GODDAMN DICK AWAY. I CAN'T FUCKING BELIEVE THIS. I HAVE SEEN IT FUCKING ALL. HOLY SHIT! FUCK! FUCK!"*

The DS poked his head out the window. "I HAVE SEEN IT ALL. THAT IS IT. I CAN RETIRE."

DRILL SERGEANTS DON'T ONLY GET INSIDE
YOUR HEAD . . . . . .

"I'M GOING TO LEVITATE AND FALL ASLEEP INSIDE YOUR SOUL!"

"PRIVATES, I WOKE UP THIS MORNING AND LOOKED IN THE MIRROR AND REALIZED THERE WERE TWO BAD MOTHERFUCKERS IN THIS WORLD

... AND I'M BOTH OF THEM."

SAVE ME! I CAN'T TAKE THIS ANYMORE...

We were outside the gas chamber right after the DS had given us our safety brief, waiting for our turn to mask up and go inside. We were having one of the few moments when we were alone as a troop, with the opportunity to sit around and shoot the shit. The DS's were fucking with the platoons ahead of us and laughing their asses off as the other troops exited the double doors. We got the chance to talk to a few of the guys who had gone through—a few said it's not so bad, others compared it to the worst experience of their lives.

Well, one private, let's call him Pvt. Dumb, was talking shit like nothing else. He was saying shit like "Oh, it can't be that bad" and "I bet I could do PT through that shit." Well, our time came and what happened will stay ingrained in my head for eternity. In fact, I hope it is the last scene I see on my deathbed so I can die laughing.

As we entered the door, Pvt. Dumb immediately started to realize that this shit burns your skin a little. He started freaking out and everyone could see the distress on his face. The DS's lined us all up against the wall and made us remove our masks one by one and recite our Social Security numbers. This was moments after the DS's explained, for the thousandth time, how to clear the mask after putting it on. Pvt. Dumb barely made it through this part and thought we had finished the process.

Next, the DS's lined us up in formation on top of a shit ton of mucus and puke. Again we were told to remove our masks. This time we would begin exercising in cadence for thirty seconds. Each section would remove their masks, do their exercise, and exit the door, and then the next section would step forward and wait for their command to do the same. Fortunately I was in the rear and got the opportunity to watch Pvt. Dumb.

Pvt. Dumb removed his mask and started wigging the fuck out. He lost control of himself and tried putting his mask back on. Only he forgot to clear it. He fell to his knees and started screaming, *"SAVE ME, SAVE ME. I CAN'T TAKE THIS ANYMORE,"* and I couldn't help but smile. The DS inside the chamber ran up to PVT Dumb while he was on his knees screaming and crying. His hands, face, and uniform were covered in the mucus and puke from the guys before us. The DS says to him, "Man the fuck up, Scout. Remember what we told you and put your mask back on and step to the back of the line. What is your problem, you pussy-fuck piece of shit?"

Pvt. Dumb tried his best to get the mask back on without success. So he threw the mask like a baseball at the DS and continued to cry like a baby (almost thirty seconds without a mask). At this point the DS decided to have a little fun. He told the Pvt. to ask the GOD of

every religion to save him before he would help him don the mask correctly. Pvt. Dumb started screaming, *"JE-SUS, BUDDHA, MUHAMMED, ALLAH, please help me! Save me!"*

The DS was laughing his ass off and said, "You're forgetting one, Pvt.!"

Pvt. Dumb is frantic at this point and said, *"WHO?"*

The DS said, *"TOM CRUISE!"*

PVT Dumb screamed, *"SAVE ME, TOM CRUISE!!!"* and just lay down and started crying.

He was snatched outside and made to go through the whole process again. Not even Tom Cruise can save you from a drill sergeant . . .

DRILL SERGEANTS LOVE TO TAKE THEIR TIME . . .

"YOU THINK THIS IS BAD, PRIVATES. THIS SESSION IS JUST THE FOREPLAY; THE REAL STUFF IS LATER."

"I SWEAR, IF YOU FAIL THIS, I WILL SLAP YOU, THEN JESUS WILL APPEAR AND SLAP YOU FOR FAILING."

**AND DON'T THINK ABOUT TOUCHING A DRILL
SERGEANT'S STUFF . . .**

"IF ANY OF YOU DIPSHITS TOUCH MY FUCKING HAT, YOU WILL BURST INTO FUCKING FLAMES!"

PART THREE
LIFE AFTER BASIC

Drill sergeants remain a part of a soldier's life long after Basic Training. Everything a drill sergeant says and does during Basic is focused on preparing a recruit to succeed in the real world—both on active duty and in life after.

Sometimes the recruits do not realize a drill sergeant's motive while they are facedown in the mud doing push-ups. But rest assured—there is a plan behind all of that yelling, cursing, and perceived abuse. Sometimes it has to be seen from a different perspective.

"How am I supposed to unfuck eighteen years in three months?" is a question you will hear often from a drill sergeant. While it is funny, it is a very accurate appraisal of the magnitude of the job they face. They have ten weeks to take a group of individuals with varied backgrounds and personalities and break them down and rebuild them as professional soldiers who operate as a team, understand the Army values, know how to shoot, move, and communicate, solve problems, and put the welfare of their fellow soldiers, Army, and ultimately the United States of America above their own before they leave for Advanced Individual Training (AIT) and begin to learn the specifics of their chosen Army Military Occupation Specialties (MOS) and then are assigned to a line unit.

For more than ten years following 9/11, it was almost a certainty that within a year privates graduating Basic Training would be deploying to Iraq or Afghanistan and find themselves in very real danger.

When graduation approaches, a lot of the things your drill sergeants said or did during your time in Basic Training, stuff that either didn't make sense or you didn't understand the importance of, starts to become more clear. For example, when I was in Basic I was in the chow hall and the private across from me was about to take a bite out of the banana he had just peeled and was holding in one hand. Out of nowhere a drill sergeant appeared and yelled, "BOTH HANDS ON THAT BANANA, YOU!" and then walked off, leaving the private thoroughly confused as he put his other hand on the banana before eating it. I had forgotten about the incident until later on in the cycle when, during a ruck march, up ahead I heard the same drill sergeant yell, "BOTH HANDS ON THAT WEAPON, YOU!" at a private who was apparently marching with only one hand holding his rifle. Then it clicked. There is a reason for everything your drill sergeant says . . . even if it seems crazy at the time.

And then, just like that . . . graduation. Holy shit! You made it. Where did the time go? It is a proud day as you march in review in front of your family and friends. You may even start to relax, to think it is safe to goof off or to let your guard down. That would be a mistake, as everywhere you go there is a drill sergeant there . . . and they can still scuff you up, and will.

DRILL SERGEANTS THINK YOU LEARNED QUITE A BIT IN TEN WEEKS . . .

"YOU'RE NOTHING BUT A ROCK WITH LIPS."

DRILL SERGEANTS CAN SHOW AFFECTION . . .

"HAVE I TOLD YOU I HATE YOU TODAY?"

DRILL SERGEANTS BELIEVE IN YOUR
NATURAL ABILITY . . .

"HEY THERE, SOLDIER, HAVE YOU ALWAYS BEEN A PUSSY OR DID YOU HAVE TO WORK TO BECOME ONE?"

**DRILL SERGEANTS KNOW HOW THE
BRAIN WORKS . . .**

"SON, YOU ARE DOWN TO ONLY TWO BRAIN CELLS LEFT. ONE'S LOST AND THE OTHER'S LOOKING FOR IT."

"I WILL CRAWL INTO YOUR MOUTH AND SHIT ON YOUR SOUL!"

**DRILL SERGEANTS VALUE THE PRINCIPLES
OF LEADERSHIP . . .**

"TO BE A LEADER
YOU HAVE TO
BE A DICK,
FIRM BUT FLEXIBLE,
PRIVATES!"

DOES YOUR DADDY HATE YOU, PRIVATE . . . ?

I come from a long line of military men, all infantry types, except for me, who went 19D cavalry scout. For those of you who don't know scout, school is sixteen weeks OSUT (One Station Unit Training). So that means sixteen weeks of the same drill sergeants. One whose name rhymed with pansy.

It was approximately week ten and so far I had managed to fly under the radar. I figured if I could keep quiet and stay out of the way, I wouldn't be paid any "special attention." We were on the ready line for mail call when our SDS picked up a package and looked at me and smiled the most menacing smile I had, or have to this day, ever seen. He put the package to the side, and when he had finished mail call, he told us to go form up for evening chow.

After about forty-five minutes of standing in formation, the troop's drill sergeant came walking out of the barracks to take us to chow. I was in the last row of Third Platoon's formation when Second Platoon's SDS came up behind me and whispered in my ear, "I'm going to fucking enjoy this." My blood ran cold . . .

I remember trying to think of what I had messed up or why he would say that to me. My platoon's SDS took charge of the troop's formation and yelled, *TROOP, AT- TENTION! PRIVATE R, POST!"*

I stood there for a split second, confused. Had he just called my name? What was going on?

"I SAID, 'POST,' GODDAMMIT!"

I was completely numb, but somehow found my way to the front of the troop.

SDS: WHY DON'T YOU TELL THE TROOP WHAT WE WERE DOING JUST BEFORE FORMATION?

ME: MAIL CALL, DRILL SERGEANT.

SDS: DID YOU GET ANY MAIL, PRIVATE?

ME: NO, DRILL SERGEANT.

SDS: WELL, I DID.

The SDS said, "Why don't you go ahead and read this to the troop." He handed me the package that I had seen during mail call earlier and I reached in, and while I was pulling out the letter . . . a baby blanket, a pacifier, and a teddy bear fell out.

Fuck. My. Life.

Dear Mr. Drill Sergeant,

Thank you so much for watching after my very special boy while he attends what he calls Day Camp. He says that his SDS is a pansy, what does he mean

by that? He left in such a hurry that he forgot to pack
properly. He left behind his binky, his blanky, and
Mr. Boo Boo. Will you please make sure that he gets
these items? I sure would appreciate it.

With love,

His Daddy

While I was reading the letter the privates in formation were trying their hardest not to bust up laughing, but were failing horribly. The other DS's were making their catcalls at me.

MY SDS: DOES YOUR "DADDY" HATE YOU, PRIVATE?

I was completely mortified.

ME: N-N-NO, DRILL SERGEANT.

During the chow line and every day until graduation I had to walk around with a pacifier in my mouth, that damn blanket draped over my shoulder, and holding Mr. Boo Boo's hand. He had become my new Battle Buddy.

A couple days later I had a chance to call my dad, and when I told him what had happened I had to listen to him laugh uncontrollably until my time on the phone was up.

All these years later I still look back on that experience and laugh my ass off, but back then I probably would have killed my own father.

YOU MAY HAVE COME A LONG WAY, BUT DRILL
SERGEANTS KNOW IT'S A LONG ROAD . . .

"YOU THINK YOU'RE STRONG ENOUGH TO WHIP MY ASS? YOU AIN'T STRONG ENOUGH TO WIPE MY ASS!"

YOUR DRILL SERGEANTS WANT YOU TO KNOW THEY ARE AT THE TOP OF THEIR GAME...

"PRIVATE, I AM A U.S. ARMY DRILL SERGEANT. I WAKE UP AND PISS EXCELLENCE."

DRILL SERGEANTS ENCOURAGE THE USE
OF PROTECTION . . .

"PRIVATES, YOU BETTER FIND A CONDOM FOR YOUR HEART, BECAUSE I'M ABOUT TO FUCK YOUR FEELINGS!"

YOUR DRILL SERGEANT WANTS YOU TO DRESS FOR SUCCESS IN LIFE . . .

"IF YOU DON'T TIGHTEN UP THAT BELT, I'M GONNA TAKE IT OFF YOUR WAIST AND WRAP IT AROUND YOUR GODDAMN NECK!"

YOUR DRILL SERGEANT STILL LIKES
COMPLIMENTING YOU ON YOUR APPEARANCE . . .

"PRIVATE, YOU LOOK LIKE HAMMERED WOLF PUSSY."

TOP TEN THINGS YOU ARE UGLIER THAN

10. A jarful of pickled assholes.

9. Three gallons of spilled fuck.

8. A bulldog with a mouth full of mayonnaise.

7. A wart on a frog's ball sack.

6. Mud flaps on a Ferrari.

5. Gary Busey and Roseanne's love child.

4. A hen's asshole in a northwest wind.

3. A painting done by Picasso on meth.

2. A stripper in West Virginia on a Wednesday afternoon.

1. A sloth that head-butted a belt sander.

DRILL SERGEANTS KNOW HOW TO
DELIVER NEWS . . .

"WELL, I HAVE GOOD NEWS AND I HAVE BAD NEWS. **GOOD NEWS** IS I SAVED FIFTEEN PERCENT OR MORE ON CAR INSURANCE JUST NOW. **BAD NEWS,** I'M ABOUT TO SMOKE THE DOG SHIT OUT OF YOU ALL AFTER CHOW."

DRILL SERGEANTS CAN QUOTE SCRIPTURE
ON THE FLY . . .

"JESUS H. TITTY FUCKING CHRIST, MARY, JOSEPH, AND THE SHEPHERDS JUMPING ON A FUCKING POGO STICK, PRIVATE!"

DRILL SERGEANTS HAVE A SPECIFIC DIET AND
EXERCISE PLAN . . .

"PRIVATES, ALL I DO IS EAT GUNPOWDER AND RUN."

DRILL SERGEANTS WANT YOU TO STAY HYDRATED . . .

"I WILL KICK YOU IN THE ASS SO HARD THE WATER ON MY KNEES WILL QUENCH YOUR THIRST!"

"PRIVATES, I HAVE TEA-BAGGED BEAR TRAPS. DO NOT PISS ME OFF."

DRILL SERGEANTS ALWAYS GET EVEN . . .

During Basic I had the responsibility of being a squad leader (SL) first, and eventually the platoon guide (PG). One of my squad members in a troop I won't ever forget was named Private K. In Basic, we are all scum and referred to as "Private."

Private K was Chinese, and did something I am still dumbfounded by today. When Private K would do some stupid shit or get into trouble, he almost always managed to get out of it. The reason being his English was fuckin' awful! He would just confuse the shit out of the DS. For instance, we were getting ready for personal time and Private K had already hit his rack and was writing a letter. DS came in, we called, "AT EASE!" and Private K jumped up quickly. DS saw him and made a beeline to him.

DS: PRIVATE K! WHAT THE FUCK ARE YOU DOING?

PRIVATE K: YESH, DRIWL SHARGENT!

With a puzzled look on his face, DS looked around and asked, "Any of you assholes speak Chinese?" He was met with silence and heads shaking. He turns to Private K and said, "Listen, fuckhead! Push-ups, you do them. No more writing letters on my fuckin time!" He emphasized his point with hand signals and facial expressions.

Private K thundered back, "YESH, DRIWL SHARGENT!" Private K still just stood there locked at parade rest.

DS was now laughing pretty much over it, and not wanting to deal with him anymore, he told us we were "fucking morons" and we had "better figure a way to square Private K away."

From that day on he pretty much just avoided Private K or having to deal with him due to his inability to keep a straight face when he yelled at Private K or when Private K talked.

The best part came graduation day. It turned out Private K spoke a dozen languages fluently including English! He also was an Officer Candidate School (OCS) candidate with two master's degrees. He was talking with all of us privates in fluent English as we all busted up laughing in complete shock that this little dude just managed to go thirteen weeks and have every single one of us believe he didn't speak much English.

Our DS heard Private K speaking fluent English as he walked by and came storming over with a look on his face that would have turned Medusa to stone. *"YOU LIT-TLE SQUIRMY MOTHERFUCKER! YOU TRICKSTER ASS DIRTY SON OF A BITCH! GUESS WHAT, FUCKHEAD, YOU LET THE CAT OUT OF THE BAG TOO SOON! YOUR BUS DOESN'T LEAVE TILL 0645 TOMORROW MORN-*

*ING AND I PROMISE YOU LITTLE SNAKE YOU AIN'T
SLEEPING A FUCKIN' BIT BETWEEN NOW AND THEN!
YOU OWE ME A SHITLOAD OF PUSH-UPS!"*

He stormed off cursing in what appeared to be nine different languages to tell the other drill sergeants about Private K's fuckery. They all pulled CQ (Charge of Quarters) that night and we could hear Private K out on the pad all night, getting thirteen weeks of pain all in one night.

**DRILL SERGEANTS ALWAYS HAVE
LIFE ADVICE . . .**

"HEY, GUY! UNFUCK YOUR LIFE!"

YOUR DRILL SERGEANT WILL LET YOU KNOW WHEN
YOU ARE OUT OF PLACE . . .

"YOU STICK OUT LIKE A DICK ON A WEDDING CAKE, PRIVATE!"

DRILL SERGEANTS LOVE HELPING YOU IMPROVE
YOUR MEMORY . . .

"WHAT THE MIND FORGETS, THE BODY MAKES UP FOR WITH CONSTANT REPETITION, PRIVATES. FRONT LEANING REST POSITION . . . MOVE!"

DRILL SERGEANTS ENCOURAGE CREATIVE THINKING . . .

"NEVER HOLD A FART IN BECAUSE IF YOU DO IT GOES UP TO YOUR BRAIN AND THAT'S HOW YOU GET SHITTY IDEAS."

EVEN NEAR GRADUATION, DRILL SERGEANTS KNOW WHO'S IN CHARGE . . .

"YOU MAY BE SMARTER THAN ME, BUT I CAN STILL FEED YOU YOUR TEETH."

DON'T FALL ASLEEP . . .

It was a Sunday and everyone was in the bay. Our drill sergeants tended to be occupied with other things and would leave us alone as long as we were doing something productive (shining boots, squaring away lockers, etc.). There was only one rule: DON'T FALL ASLEEP. I was sitting on my bunk—I forget what I was doing—and I noticed that a troop two racks over had nodded off. I thought that I should wake up the offending private when I saw one of the drill sergeants from B Company (we were A Company) creeping across our bay.

This particular DS was the only one in the battalion with a ranger tab and had a look that could freeze your blood. He saw me see him, gave me a death look, and put a finger to his lips. I could only watch as he crept toward the now snoring private. Silently he produced a canteen, unscrewed it, and poured its contents on Sleepy's head. Sleepy woke up, sputtering and swinging his arms, then DS Ranger Tab pushed him down into his rack and said something that still makes me laugh.

DS Ranger Tab got about a centimeter from Sleepy's face and said, "Go back to sleep, Private. It was only a WET DREAM!"

Another time, me and a Battle Buddy had come down on Charge of Quarters in the Company Training Area of the Basic Training barracks at the shitty hours of 0200 to

0400. One of us got the bright idea that we would take short naps in shifts. My buddy put his head down and passed out immediately while I kept watch. Soon after, I became bored and kicked my chair back on the rear legs and against the wall behind me. I guess I nodded off pretty quickly after that, as my head assumed the same position—kicked back against the wall, mouth open, and snoring, I'm sure.

I don't know how long I was out for, or for what reason I woke up, but when I opened my eyes there was our senior DS looming in front of me with his index finger extended and fully in my mouth but not touching anything . . . staring me dead in the face.

It must have been only twenty to thirty seconds, but it felt like an eternity before DS removed his finger and while staring deep into my soul quietly said, "You're lucky it was my finger, Joe . . ."

Lesson learned about falling asleep on watch! Well played, DS . . . Well played.

YOUR DRILL SERGEANT REALLY DOES WANT YOU TO SHUT THE FUCK UP . . .

"PRIVATE, SHUT THE FUCK UP OR I'LL TAKE YOUR BOTTOM LIP, STRETCH IT OVER YOUR FOREHEAD, AND SUFFOCATE YOU WITH IT."

AND YOUR DRILL SERGEANT REALLY DOES WANT
YOU OUT OF HIS FACE . . .

"DO AN ABOUT-FACE, A LEFT FACE, AND GET OUTTA MY FACE."

"I SWEAR TO GOD,
PRIVATES,
BRM ISN'T THAT HARD!
I'VE BEEN TELLING
YOU THIS UNTIL I'M
BLUE IN THE FACE,
AND YOU STILL
DON'T GET IT.
I'M TELLING YOU,
I'M GONNA BE NINETY
YEARS OLD,
ON MY DEATHBED
OR SOME SHIT,

AND MY GREAT-
GRANDKIDS ARE GONNA
HEAR ME WHISPERING
SOMETHING.
'WHAT IS IT, POP-POP?'
THEY'RE GONNA ASK AS
THEY LEAN DOWN, AND
ALL THEY'RE GONNA
HEAR IS ME SAYING,
'PRIVATE,
PUT YOUR GODDAMN
NOSE TO THE
FUCKING CHARGING
HANDLE!'"

YOU SHOULD REALLY GIVE YOUR DRILL SERGEANT
SOME SPACE . . .

"PRIVATE, GO AWAY, YOU SMELL LIKE FAILURE AND CORN CHIPS."

PLANNING FOR THE FUTURE . . .

DS: WHAT DO YOU WANT OUT OF LIFE?

PRIVATE: I WOULD LOVE TO HAVE A PIECE OF PROPERTY TO CALL MY OWN ONE DAY.

DS: SEE THAT PATCH OF GRASS OVER THERE?

PRIVATE: YES, DRILL SERGEANT.

DS: UNTIL THE DAY YOU GRADUATE, IF YOU ARE LUCKY ENOUGH TO GRADUATE, THAT IS YOUR PROPERTY. NOW GET OVER THERE AND FRONT BACK GO UNTIL THE GRASS IS GONE. MOVE!

The day I graduated Basic there was no grass in "my" spot. Parents took pictures.

YOUR DRILL SERGEANT WANTS YOU TO KNOW
YOU AREN'T GONE YET . . .

"YOU AREN'T OFFICIALLY GONE UNTIL YOU EAT IT HERE AND SHIT IT THERE."

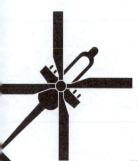

"YOUR MOTHERS
AND SISTERS
WON'T BE CRYING
ON GRADUATION DAY
BECAUSE THEY'RE
HAPPY TO SEE YOU.
THEY'LL BE CRYING
BECAUSE THEY SAW MY
WEDDING RING."

IF YOU WORK HARD ENOUGH, YOUR DRILL
SERGEANT MAY EVEN COMPLIMENT YOU . . .

"YOU PRIVATES ARE ALL RIGHT. EXCEPT YOU. YOU SUCK."

PUT IN THE EFFORT AND YOUR DRILL SERGEANT
WILL PUSH YOU THAT EXTRA MILE . . .

"I WILL PUNT
YOU THROUGH
THE GOALPOST
OF LIFE!"

A DRILL SERGEANT AS SEEN BY
AN ARMY MOM . . .

On May 29, 2010, my daughter graduated high school. Two days later, on June 1, 2010, she was on her way to Basic Combat Training (BCT). She was a mousy kid, introverted. She lived in her own little bubble because it was safer that way. She avoided conflict at all costs, even to her own detriment.

The letters started coming home quickly. She was distraught. She wanted to come home. She was miserable. She thought she'd made the wrong decision. Of course, as a mom . . . I was freaking out! I went to a close friend of the family, a retired brig. gen. that had watched my daughter grow up. He just smiled, sighed, and said, "Settle down, Mom. Those drill sergeants have got this thing down to a science."

Slowly but surely, the letters started getting a little better. She was still homesick and still terrified, but there was a hint of a new happiness in those letters that seemed rooted in discovering teamwork and trusting others.

By the end of White Phase, the letters started sounding confident. She joked. She teased about DS "T" going batshit crazy on houseflies when she saw them and DS "R" having an evil sense of humor. During the last week or two of BCT, she said: "This is the best decision I ever made."

I still read through all those letters. I still marvel at the change. I've read through them probably twenty times and I'm still stunned at the change.

When we went to her BCT graduation at Fort Leonard Wood, I was amazed when I saw my once mousy, introverted daughter. She was standing straight and tall, her jaw was squarely set. She was in rock-solid physical condition, and best of all . . . she was smiling. She was looking people in the eye. She was proud to wear that uniform.

To this mom . . . watching the whole thing unfold through letters, a drill sergeant is a potter with an impossible job. He or she has several lumps of clay lying in front of them. All of those lumps have different textures and degrees of coarseness. Some are easier to mold than others. But it's up to the DS to mold, shape, and fire all of those lumps of clay into solid, finished work. And he has to do it all simultaneously. He has to take the raw, coarse lump and mold it at the same time as he's molding a more pliable, smooth lump. It takes a special breed of cat to pull that one off.

To this day, my daughter views her drill sergeants as some of the most important people she's met in her life. In fact, in many ways . . . she views y'all as having given her life. Or giving her life quality, at least.

One of y'all even gave her a nickname that sticks with her to this day: "Squidget" (1/2 Squirt + 1/2 Midget = Squidget).

Thank you. Thank you for knowing when she needed an "in your face, asshole," when she needed an "atta girl," and when she just needed to feel a part of. Y'all are amazing.

DRILL SERGEANTS KNOW WHAT LIFE AFTER BASIC
IS REALLY ABOUT . . .

"PRIVATES, THERE ARE TWO THINGS IN LIFE YOU CANNOT ESCAPE: DEATH AND TAXES. NOW, I CAN'T KILL YOU, BUT I WILL GET MY TAXES! FRONT LEANING REST POSITION, MOVE!"

"WHAT THE FUCK IS WRONG WITH YOU, PRIVATE?! I HAVE A DEGREE IN FUCKING PSYCHOLOGY! I WILL MIND-FUCK YOU!

TEN YEARS FROM NOW I WON'T EVEN REMEMBER YOU, BUT YOU'LL STILL BE A CONTORTED LITTLE SHIT BECAUSE OF THE THINGS I'M ABOUT TO DO TO YOU!"

DRILL SERGEANTS WANT YOU TO UNDERSTAND
HOW THE GOVERNMENT REALLY WORKS . . .

"THE ARMY IS NOT
A DEMOCRACY.
IT IS A DICTATORSHIP
THAT DEFENDS
AND ALLOWS FOR A
DEMOCRACY . . .
AND I AM THE DICTATOR.
NOW PUSH!"

DRILL SERGEANTS KNOW HOW TO LEAVE A MARK . . .

"I AM GOING TO KICK YOU IN YOUR CHEST PLATE SO FUCKING HARD YOUR FUCKING GREAT-GRANDKIDS WILL HAVE MY BOOT PRINT AS A BIRTHMARK! BEAT YOUR FUCKING FACE!"

SOMETIMES, YOU CAN ACTUALLY IMPRESS
A DRILL SERGEANT . . .

"PRIVATE,
I USED TO THINK
YOU WERE THE
MOST USELESS
HUMAN BEING I HAD
COME ACROSS IN
ALL MY YEARS
ON THIS EARTH.
BUT THEN I REALIZED
THAT YOU ARE A
BEACON OF HOPE."

THE TRUE ESSENCE OF THE DRILL SERGEANT

This story isn't about my own basic training, but rather that of a WWII Veteran. I met him post-OSUT graduation at the National Infantry Museum, where he was working, a few years ago. I often think about what he said to me that day . . .

"WE COULDN'T UNDERSTAND WHY THE DRILL SERGEANTS HATED US, WE WERE JUST KIDS. WE DIDN'T KNOW WHY THEY CONSTANTLY SCREAMED AT US, AND RAN US TO EXHAUSTION. THEY WERE THE MEANEST BASTARDS I EVER HAD THE DISPLEASURE OF KNOWING. SOON AFTER THAT I TOO WENT TO EUROPE, AND THERE I REALIZED SOMETHING ABOUT DRILL SERGEANTS. THEY DIDN'T HATE US, THEY CARED ABOUT US MORE THAN WE COULD EVER IMAGINE. THEY KNEW SOMETHING WE DIDN'T. THEY HAD FOUGHT THE NAZIS, AND SEEN THEIR FRIENDS DIE. THEY TREATED US THE WAY THEY DID . . . BECAUSE THEY KNEW WE WEREN'T READY."

ACKNOWLEDGMENTS

What a whirlwind this has been. There are a number of things I know how to do—putting together a book with a large national publisher was not one of them. I want to thank HarperCollins and Dey Street Books for giving me the opportunity to bring what we do at ASMDSS and Battle in Distress to the national forum. To my editors, first Mark and then Brittany, thank you for bearing with me and spending so much time walking me through the process.

A big thanks to the fans who have continued to engage with us and share their experiences. Since the beginning ASMDSS has focused on sharing the stories submitted by fans who want the public to know of their experiences.

To the page admins, moderators and our web development team, I could not have done or continue to do any of this without your help and dedication. Thank you.

RESOURCES

A nation is judged on how they treat their warriors once they return from the field of battle. Despite our best intentions and efforts as a society, we are failing those who sacrificed for us in exchange for the unspoken promise that we, as a nation, would have their back when the fighting was done.

—DAN CADDY, FOUNDER OF BATTLE IN DISTRESS, INC.

The ASMDSS Facebook page that inspired this book is not just fun and games and hilarious (and painful) drill sergeant stories. The ASMDSS community is so much more. In addition to donating and raising funds for veterans in need and supporting military charities, ASMDSS has been able to use our reach to connect those who want to help with those in need. For me the most amazing and life changing thing to come out of ASMDSS, beyond the laughs, was the creation of Battle in Distress.

Battle in Distress, Inc., was born of a serious flaw in our national thinking towards assisting veterans. As a nation, we have many resources available to veterans returning home. Organizations are in place to assist with mental health, housing, financial concerns, physical health, job training, and dozens of other categories. The common theme of these organizations is the requirement for the veteran to navigate a web of forms, requirements, procedures, and automated phone systems in order to receive help. How can we expect those who sacrificed and fought for our country to return home and take up another battle to receive the benefits and services they need and have earned? Battle in distress is a resource for modern veterans that harnesses the power of social media and uses it as a way to connect warfighters across the country who share the common bond of serving their country yet face the challenge of returning home alone. Battle in Distress, Inc., was launched on January 15, 2013, to serve as a strong support system to those brave men and women who answered the call, stood up, and served our nation. As we see it, our duty at Battle in Distress is to ensure that all service members, whether active or retired, know that no matter what they may face in their daily lives, they're never alone. All a battle needs to do is reach out to our organization. We will take the fight from there and provide a three-tiered response system to provide resources suited to the veteran's individual needs.

I first recognized the problem within our existing system by looking at how we treat veterans with PTSD and suicidal thoughts. I saw that suicide was not the problem. What I saw was suicide becoming a result of problems stacking up in a veteran's life until they become too difficult to face. There are plenty of resources available for veterans contemplating suicide, but why are we waiting until men and women are suicidal before attempting to connect them with help? It is our belief at Battle in Distress that if we are waiting for our veterans to consider taking their own lives, we have failed. The problem should be confronted long before suicide enters the picture. There is no excuse for denying a veteran the assistance they require until they are so desperate that they consider hurting themselves.

For us, the solution to the problem does not lie within expensive government programs. Military service members hold the solution within themselves. Battle In Distress, Inc., focuses on rallying the brotherhood of service members to its full might to help to confront the seemingly minor issues in our veteran's lives that, if left unchecked, grow into the big problems.

Battle in Distress offers a place for troops to stand up and stand together to take care of their own. It is time for our troops to strengthen their bonds and secure the future of anybody who bravely answered the call to serve our nation, the United States of America.

As a good friend of mine, Boone Cutler, says, "Every Warfighter needs two things to survive, a Battle Buddy and a mission." By getting warfighters who are in distress connected to fellow warfighters looking to help, we are helping to give them the two things needed for them to overcome any obstacle.

Battle in Distress is formed of highly motivated volunteers who are all either active duty service members or veterans. The volunteers' mission is to walk beside the veteran or service member who is currently overwhelmed with their current situation, re-engaging them in the warfighter community as well as linking them up with the proper resource in order to get them the specific help they need.

We use crisis intervention training and our CAD's resource database, which currently contains over 200,000 resources throughout the country. Battle in Distress uses this database to establish and maintain specific points of contact with the listed resources. Our system sends out automated correspondence with the resources listed in order to maintain a detailed and accurate list of requirements, hours of operation, and specific starting points to receive benefits. This method is unique in the fact that we are not simply using Google and dropping phone numbers, but are linking up our veterans and service members in real time with the specific person and organization that will help them achieve their goals of coming out of the darkness and back into the light.

Since 2012, Battle in Distress has worked more than five thousand calls for service, ALL of which have been successfully resolved. In the beginning stages of the organization, the vast number of our calls were cases where the soldier was facing suicidal thoughts. As the word of our mission continues to successfully spread, the number of our suicide cases continues to drop. But just one is still too many. Our highly motivated and trained staff of professionals is working relentlessly to make sure that number go to, and stays at, zero. At Battle in Distress you do not walk alone.

> *"I'd carry you through the flames of hell, my flesh burned to the bone. Through the places where the demons dwell, you'll never be alone. We are your Battles, now and always, you never walk alone."*

If you or someone you know is in distress or needs assistance, please contact our Battle Response Team (BRT) via a message to our Facebook page at http://www.facebook.com/BattleInDistress

To learn more about us or volunteer for Battle in Distress, please visit our website at http://www.battleindistress.org

ABOUT THE AUTHOR

DAN CADDY is a former marketing professional and veteran of Operation Enduring Freedom. He is the founder of the Awesome Sh*t My Drill Sergeant Said Facebook page. The Facebook page now has more than ten individuals on staff, including many current and former drill sergeants. Dan is the president and founder of Battle in Distress Inc., a nonprofit devoted to helping service members in crisis. He lives in Vermont and continues to serve in the military.